THE ANTI-VILLAIN LEAGUE
-HANDBOOK-

Adapted by D. Jakobs

Based on the Motion Picture Screenplay
Written by Cinco Paul & Ken Daurio

Little, Brown and Company
New York • Boston

Table of Contents

MEMO

You hold in your hands a thorough guide to the world-famous, completely secret Anti-Villain League, the Earth's greatest defense against its most cunning inhabitants. There are super villains who would do anything to snatch this book from your hands—never to be seen again until they reemerge in a dastardly attempt to use this information to fill the Grand Canyon or enact some other large-scale mayhem. **DO NOT ALLOW THIS TO HAPPEN.**

Oh, and by simply picking up this volume, your chemical profile has been logged into our system. So don't even think about pulling any fast ones.

A PEEK INSIDE

Here's a glimpse, a glance, a very quick peek at some of the people and places that make up the Anti-Villain League. Don't look too closely—this is highly confidential information! In fact, would you mind putting your hand in front of your eyes as you read this section?

Silas Ramsbottom: The Man with the Plan

"We are the Anti-Villain League, an ultra-secret organization dedicated to fighting crime on a global scale. Rob a bank? We're not interested. Kill someone? Not our deal. But you want to melt the polar ice caps? Or vaporize Mount Fuji? Or steal the moon? Then we notice."

—Silas Ramsbottom, director of the AVL

Silas Ramsbottom of the East London Ramsbottom. Excuse me? There's nothing funny about that. He has proudly led the Anti-Villain League for an entirely secret number of years. Not Sheepsbutt, not Goatsheinie, and certainly not Lambsbooty!

Silas Ramsbottom. Remember the name. Now forget it! He is the director of a top secret organization, for goodness' sake.

Where in the World Is the AVL?

This map shows where all the Anti-Villain League offices are located worldwide. Stop by and see us sometime…if you can find us! You think we would actually give you a map? We're secret spies, after all!

Cupcake Battler!!!

Our agents have had to fight many things—sharks, dastardly masterminds, brainwashed monkeys, bigger sharks, sentient cookie robots, you name it. So you never know when there may be some dangerous baked goods lurking. We always prepare our agents to be able to eliminate all dangerous baked goods from an area—because batter happens, folks. Lucy Wilde, one of our most dutifully trained operatives, can destroy an entire bakery full of cupcakes in fewer than seven seconds. In doing so, she not only set the world record for massive cupcake destruction but also for messiest bakery ever. She uses a combination of jujitsu, Krav Maga, Aztec warfare, and krumping. It's not pretty, but it gets the job done.

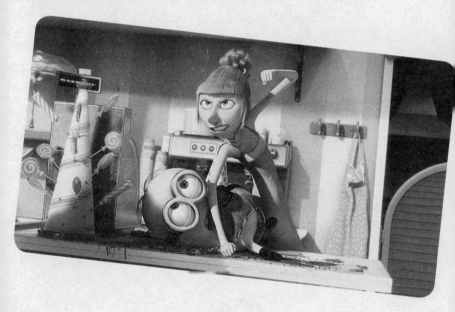

We Love Lucy

"You know, I could rip your heart out of your chest and show it to you if I wanted to. Yeah. I saw it in a movie once, and it looked pretty easy. *Ba-boom, ba-boom, ba-boom.*"

—AVL Agent Lucy Wilde

Bake My Day

Bake My Day Cupcake Shop is but one example of the many undercover AVL spy fronts that we have installed pretty much everywhere around the globe. This top secret artistic rendering of the space will demonstrate some of our spy-mazing work.

Lamp Shade Mini–Command Center

AVL Agent Lucy Wilde

Kitchen

Good for deflecting cupcake attacks

Perfect place to hide a surveillance camera

Embeds tiny tracking devices into shoes

It Had to Be Gru

At the AVL, we recruit the best. And sometimes the best are the worst. Bear with us here. Picture the world's former number one super villain. Pretty bad, right? One might even say the worst. But when we gathered secret intelligence that this super villain's ways had been curtailed by a trio of cute orphans, we knew just what we had to do. Gru's job experience would make him one of the most qualified operatives the AVL has ever employed. He is dangerous, brilliant, and comes complete with a veritable army of tiny Minions! Gotta get Gru. Of course, he may need some convincing.

"Okay, I see where this is going with all the spy stuff, but no. No! I am a father now. And a legitimate businessman. I am developing a line of delicious jams and jellies."

—Gru

The Invitation

Sometimes Director Ramsbottom really, really, really needs someone to come down to the AVL head-quarters for a conversation. We have developed two methods for achieving this goal:

Option 1:

- Kidnap potential recruit.
- Zap into unconsciousness.
- Stuff incapacitated body into trunk of car.
- Bring to underwater submarine.

Option 2:

- Call on phone.

TIPS FROM THE BEST

We know how it is. Going up against devious super villains trying to take over the world can be difficult. Especially if you haven't been trained by the most amazing league of people-against-villains in the entire world. Lucky for you, though, the AVL is feeling amazingly generous today! Enjoy these tips from our most elite operatives.

Weapon Announcements

Sometimes you find yourself in a momentary stand-off with your foe. At times like this, it is incredibly tempting to brag about your weapon before you fire (e.g., "Ha! Freeze Ray!"). **DO NOT DO THIS.** By announcing the specs of your weapon, you are revealing an important secret to your enemy—namely that you've got a secret Freeze Ray completely hidden in your coat pocket. Consider instead holding on to the element of surprise. There is plenty of time to brag, boast, and make bad puns after the deed is done.

Let Magnets Do It for You

Magnets use forces of science to attract metal thingies. Thus, they are exceptionally useful when you need a metal thingy and do not want to bend down and pick it up. The bigger the magnet, the bigger the metal thingy you can lift. And if you have a giant magnet, you can lift ALL the metal thingies around you. But be careful as metal thingies tend to be sharp.

IMPORTANT NOTE: If using magnets to steal, be sure to return all stolen items to their rightful places when you are finished with them. If you don't, we will know. Because we're the ones telling you about how cool giant magnets are in the first place. So don't betray our trust like that.

Pint-Size Disguise

Going undercover is an important aspect of being a world-class crime fighter. Here at the AVL, we know all the tricks that will keep you from being exposed in the trickiest of situations. For instance, you may need to be undercover at a small child's birthday party. You'd be surprised how often this is the case. We recommend the disguise of a happy family of three. Throw on a wig, and have your partner tape on a mustache. Grab another agent to play Baby. No one will be the wiser!

Driving with Purpose

Any good super spy needs to know how to drive under special circumstances. For instance, let's say you just happen to have small assassins clinging to the back of your car. What would you do then? Are you prepared for such an occurrence? Our agents are! Here's a little how-to on evasive driving tactics.

1. Weave in and out of traffic like you have a bee stuck in your car. Don't hit any other cars while you are doing this.

2. Choose just the right moment and slam on the brakes. The assassins' momentum should carry them forward, up over your vehicle.

3. Open your automatic sunroof. If properly timed, the assassins will land neatly beside you on the passenger seat.

4. Zap away! Zapping is an important part of any balanced evasive action.

5. Stuff the Minions inside your glove compartment for the rest of the trip. If your glove compartment is full, consider cleaning it out once in a while. This is a company car, you know.

Keeping Up

Let's say that you are the one chasing a getaway car. There are certain supplies and skills you will need to stay on the tail of that speeding vehicle.

1. Magnets. As previously mentioned, magnets stick to metal thingies. A car is a metal thingy. Therefore, using the transitive property of stickiness, magnets stick to cars. Awfully handy if you happen to be chasing one.

2. Suspenders. This quaint fashion accessory can be crucial for strapping yourself to the rear bumper of the car in question. Do keep in mind that this will result in your being pulled behind said car at very high speeds. For this reason, we recommend you know how to...

3. Ski on a cardboard box! Cardboard boxes are easy to come across when you are being pulled behind a car at high speeds and can be used to help smooth out your ride.

4. Bed sheets. If you happen to be lucky enough to be flung into one of these, you can quickly pull it off the clothesline and use it to parasail behind the car you're chasing. The sheet's parachutelike action should carry you up into the sky and out of the danger zone. Always look out for passing geese! We can't stress this enough!

Card Conundrum

Your business cards need to have a contact number on them so potential recruits can reach you, but you don't want to write out the name of your top secret organization on them. We at the Anti-Villain League have overcome this problem by just putting down our initials (otherwise known as our acronym): AVL. The trick here is that these letters could just as easily stand for many things: Aggressive Valets Legion, Abnormal Vegetable Lawyers, or, um, well, actually, we could use a few more non-secret AVLs to have on the tips of our tongues. Please use the space below to come up with five other things *AVL* could stand for. The world will be grateful.

1. _____
2. _____
3. _____
4. _____
5. _____

It is extra-important to keep in touch with your fellow agents when you are on a mission. You may need them to crash in through the ceiling, drive up a down escalator, or blast the area with really loud compelling dance music to save you from an adventure gone awry.

Keep your communication lines open! Use phones, walkie-talkies, smoke signals, semaphore flags, or tin cans connected with twine. Whatever it takes!

Say It with Flags

Semaphore flags are a sneaky way to communicate with your allies. By holding up your signals in different positions, you spell out your message. Slowly, silently, and really just soooooo slowly. But silently!

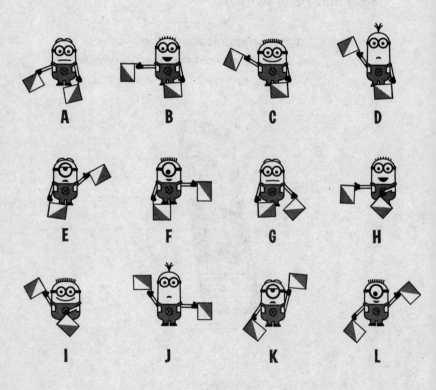

M N O P

Q R S T

U V W X

Y Z

Semaphorically Speaking

Please test your newfound Semaphorese by translating these simple statements back into English. The answers can be found on pages 69–70.

____ ____ ____ ____ ____ ____ ,

____

___ ___ ___ ___ ___ ___

___ ___ ___ ___ ___ ___

___ ___ ___!

_____ —

___ ___ ___ ___ ___ ___ .

Temporally Appropriate Clothing

At nighttime, you wear the clothes that go with the night. This is true for owls, and it's doubly true for AVL agents. Some choose black jumpsuits that blend into the dark; while others go with brightly colored clothes to blend in with the party crowd. Our own director, Silas Ramsbottom, does his best late-night work in comfy stripy flannel pj's and a floppy nightcap. To each their own, as they say.

Dry My Car

If you plan to drive a hybrid automobile-submarine, an amphibious roadster of the deep, you need a way to dry it out. To help you figure this out, we present our own ingenious solution. Down at the massive hush-hush underwater AVL headquarters, we have developed a unique way of ensuring that our own amphibious roadsters stay in top condition. When a vehicle lands, a giant hair dryer extends from a panel in the floor and proceeds to blast the car with hot air, like only a giant hair dryer can. If your hair is wet, it will even dry that for you at no extra charge. Brought to you by the unparalleled minds of the Anti-Villain League.

Tracking Footprints

Footprints are all around us. You have recently pressed your own foot down onto the floor, leaving a print invisible to the human eye—unless you stepped in something outside, in which case it's all too visible. (In fact, hey, clean that up!)

Any good agent knows how to read footprints. Here's a list of some of the footprints you should be able to recognize.

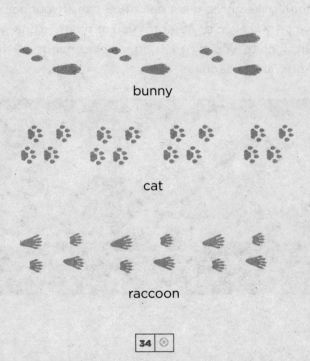

bunny

cat

raccoon

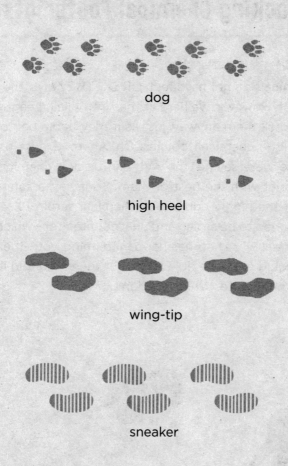

dog

high heel

wing-tip

sneaker

Minion

Tracking Chemical Footprints

Chemicals do not have feet. OR DO THEY? No, they do not. However, we here at the Anti-Villain League can track them anyway, just as if they had a pair of cute little chemical footsies. Oh. Ahem. Excuse us. As we were saying, the AVL can track a chemical footprint with the best of them. So if, say, a canister of the highly dangerous chemical serum PX-41 happened to be stolen and unaccounted for—which we are NOT saying has happened, mind you—then we would easily be able to go out there and find it. If we needed to. Which we don't.

Toupee or Not Toupee?

Sometimes the best disguise is a simple haircut. Now for our, shall we say, follicle-challenged agents, a haircut is not possible. Because they have no hair. Because they are bald. Bald as an egg of a baby bald eagle. In these extreme cases, instead of taking hair away, why not try adding hair? A wig can change anyone's profile, sometimes quite dramatically.

Grappling Hooks = Underrated

Look up. Are there any railings? Any ledges? Any scaffolding? Any heavy furniture or well-anchored overhead lights? If you answered yes to any of these questions, then it's the right place and the right time to use a grappling hook. We at the AVL always send our operatives out with at least one pair of grappling hooks jammed into their pockets. The hooks are just that handy. Here is a short guide to their use:

1. Aim well. You need to catch the hook around something, or the pointy part of the grappling hook will come hurtling back at you and may, in fact, stick into your body—and that's rarely helpful. (Though there was one time when it ended up lancing a blister, but that's another story.)

2. Wear thick pants. If you have a grappling hook in your pocket, the aforementioned pointy part can jab into your leg over and over while you walk. And that's not very comfy.

3. Swing the hook around. Our agents have found that they look much cooler if they hold on to the rope part and whip the hook around in a spinning circle before they throw it.

4. Know when to retract. AVL grappling hooks have a button on them that winds the rope, thereby pulling you (and anyone you're holding) up to the place where the hook has been lodged. You must time the button-press just right, though. If you press it too soon, it will pull the hook back at you instead. See #1.

5. Lift with your legs. Some of our agents are very heavy. If you are going to grab colleagues around the waist and carry them to safety, be sure to use your lower body to heave them up. You don't want to throw out your back, thereby ruining a glamorous getaway.

The Great Escape

It can happen to the best of us: You get stuck in a tense situation, are out of weapons and sneaky gadgets, are overmatched, and are forced to rely only on your wit as a way of getting free. Would you have any idea what to do? Each situation calls for its own well-calibrated response. However, wouldn't it be amazing if there were a strategy that you could use every time? Sometimes you're cornered by a super villain and sometimes by lions and sometimes by awkwardly threatening robots.

In light of this, the AVL has put a great deal of our considerable resources into coming up with an escape method that can *always* work. Last week, we finally masterminded it—an all-purpose strategy that could very well save your mission and your life. I share it with you now: six steps to safety.

1. Yell "Whaaaaat?????" really loudly.

2. Look around.

3. Use one hand to vaguely gesture over your shoulder.

4. Say, "I think I hear someone calling me."

5. Apologize.

6. Leave.

There is never a wrong time to use this strategy. It is perfect in its simplicity. And it always works. Because—and here's the trick—your foe won't know that there's really no one calling you! Genius. Sheer genius.

Down Under

You may be called upon to move to another country. As we just opened an office in Sydney, Australia, here are some notes on how you might fit in Down Under.

1. Didgeridoo. A tall, sticklike musical instrument that makes weird and awesome sounds. It's also a fun word to say.

2. G'day. It is always daytime in Australia. Except when it gets dark.

3. Great Barrier Reef. Large, magnificent, natural landmark—must keep an eye on this, as it seems like just the thing an Australian super villain would want to steal.

4. Marsupials. Due to divergent evolution, everything in Australia has a pouch! This especially comes in handy for storage purposes (for instance, if you need to store two kangaroos when you only have space for one).

5. Regular people. If you relocate to Australia, don't keep saying "regular people" do this or "regular people" have that. Australians seem to think that they themselves are regular people!

6. Seasons. Australians have their winter when regular people have summer, and Australians have summer when regular people have winter. Their toilets also flush backward! How silly is that?

7. Wallaby. Like a kangaroo, but smaller. They are like the Minions of the marsupial world. Only not yellow.

    With this guide, you will certainly blend right in. Good luck with your relocation!

Safecracking for Fun and Glory

Have you cracked a safe? Ah, then you know the satisfaction when all the interior wheels align and—*CLICK!*—the door slowly opens. Sure, we have developed advanced safecracking technology that automatically figures out the combinations for the most difficult high-tech safes on the planet. But there's just something about knowing how to do it the old-fashioned way that really gives you a sense of satisfaction. And then, once you crack it open, you can go ahead and grab those warm and gooey items that were locked away—salsas and serums and all that good stuff.

The most important thing in old-school safe-crackery is to use a stethoscope. Just like a doctor. Listening to the safe through the stethoscope lets you hear all the telltale pauses and clicks while you spin the combination wheel. These tiny sounds are the ones that will help you spring the lock. Plus, you can quickly tell if the safe has a chest cold. If you don't have a stethoscope, feel free to sub in a banana. It may not work as well, but it'll look funny and the Minions just love it.

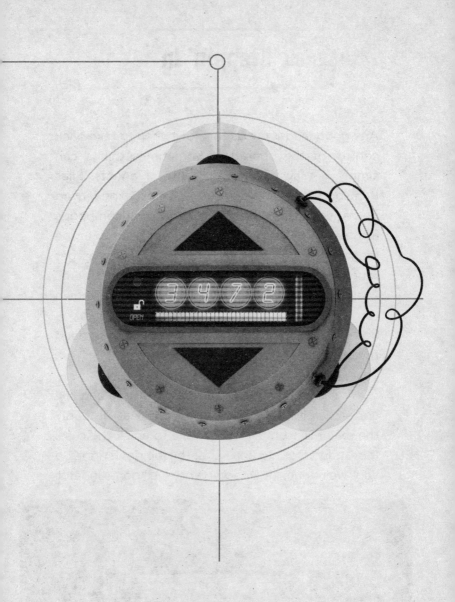

Steppin' In

Any good leader needs to know when to take back control of the operation. Sometimes things can simply get away from the best of agents. Silas Ramsbottom knows that even his most experienced operatives may in fact be bumbling nincompoops at times. It's just something you get used to in the mega-crime-fighting business. So when times get rough, directors need to get tough. If your agents keep insisting that an old super villain who is known to be deceased is behind a current crime and you know that they're completely wrong, then you need to step in and take over.

And if it turns out later that they were actually correct, well, then your intervention was probably the major reason they were able to crack the case. It prodded them to finally get the job done right. So very well done, Sir Director. Very well done, indeed.

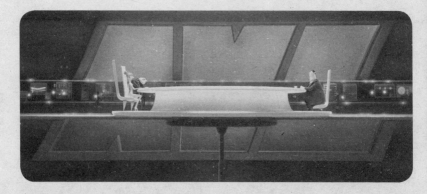

The Importance of Gathering Minions

Minions are recommended. While we here at the AVL don't use them on our own, we were more than pleased to add them to our stockpile of resources once we convinced Gru to come aboard.

They have proven themselves good for birthday parties, babysitting, cleaning, going undercover, putting out fires, testing dangerous serums, performing magic tricks, smashing things, driving getaway vehicles, clinging to grappling hooks, baking cupcakes, being really loud sirens, role-playing when you need to practice asking someone out on a date, and much, much more.

It can be tricky to understand what they're saying, but they are primarily loyal and do seem to love bashing one another on the head—which may come in handy if we can figure out a use for that.

AVL INVENTORY

The AVL has a number of items so devious and powerful that super villainy doesn't really stand a chance. This guide will now allow you to read, for the first time, descriptions of some of these items. Read them with care.

Freeze Ray

A Freeze Ray is very handy on a hot day. When properly calibrated, it will immobilize any attacker within a solid block of ice—frozen ice, that is! Bring a small chisel, and you are all set to serve frosty refreshing drinks to your pals, while your enemies cool their heels.

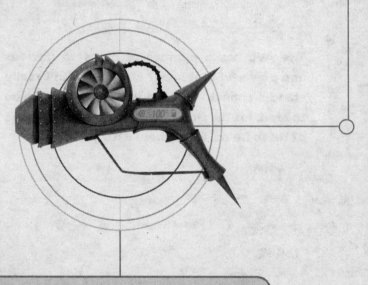

Pro: Good for parties.

Con: Not so good against Flamethrowers.

Flamethrower

Get 'em while they're hot. Flamethrowers are sizzling. Talk about painting the town red: With a Flamethrower, you can burn up anything in your path. They are extremely dangerous, though, so be sure to practice your aim—preferably somewhere safe, like in the middle of a swimming pool.

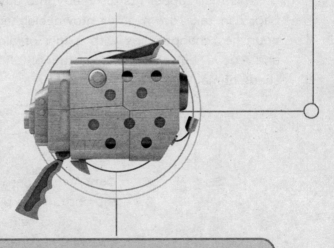

Pro: Never be scared of a scarecrow again.

Con: A simple bucket of water could signal the end of all your fiery good times.

AVL-Issued Lipstick

Lips get chapped. And sometimes chaps need to get "lipped." (Particularly if by "lipped," you mean "knocked unconscious by a surge of electricity that makes their limbs flail about painfully/hilariously.") (And we do.) (Mean that.)

This mini-zapper fits discreetly into any handbag, can take down a full-grown elephant, and nourishes chapped lips with a mix of aloe vera and cocoa butter in a devastatingly flattering shade of magenta.

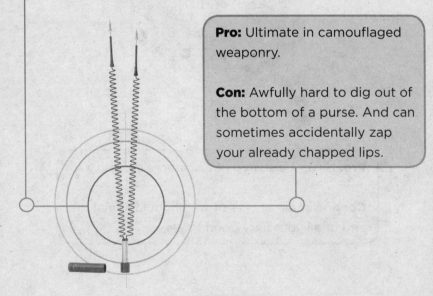

Pro: Ultimate in camouflaged weaponry.

Con: Awfully hard to dig out of the bottom of a purse. And can sometimes accidentally zap your already chapped lips.

Fart Gun

Originally invented when Dr. Nefario misheard "dart gun," the Fart Gun has taken on a life of its own the past few years. A "P.U.-tiful" feat of engineering, the gun releases a small cloud of the stinkiest gas around. It has become something of an honor to be sent off with a twenty-one Fart Gun salute— guaranteed to bring a tear to your eye, and the eyes of all those in whiffing distance.

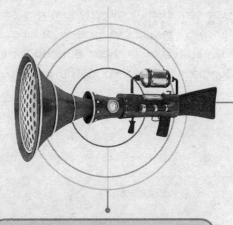

Pro: Easy to blame for your own flatulence problems.

Con: May wilt your flowers. And not usable downwind.

Lamp Shade Mini-Command Center

When our operatives are in the field, they don't have access to the cool computers in our underwater AVL command center. Instead we outfit them with a mini-command center of their own, usually hidden in a secret location in their field office, like an overhead lamp. You just stand underneath the dome and press the button to lower it down around you. The inside of the lamp shade is a fully decked-out touch screen that directly controls an array of surveillance cameras of the sneakiest kinds possible. Sure, it's a little cozy in there. But cuddle up, operatives! Cuddle in the name of battling villainy.

Pro: Stays mainly out of the way, up by the ceiling.

Con: May gather spiderwebs. And spiders! Ack!

Tracking Camera with Night Vision

You may need to take pictures in the dark. When normal people do this, they use something called a "flash." You have probably had one of these blinding lights shone in your eyes before. Not so sneaky, right? You can totally notice when one of these is used. With our night-vision camera, on the other hand, no one will know you're there. Plus, it lights up when you point it at your target to notify you that you've found what you're looking for. But don't worry; no one else can see the part that lights up when you find your target. And that's why we win the Smartest Super Villian–Fighting Agency Award year after year.

Pro: No flash!

Con: Tracking mechanism may have a difficult time identifying strange species (i.e., Gru's pet, Kyle).

X-ray Goggles

Sometimes night vision isn't enough. Sometimes you need to see right through things. Let's say you are searching a super villain's lair for a safe that holds a highly unpleasant serum. And for argument's sake, let's say you can't find the safe anywhere. And believe me, you've looked. You looked behind the paintings and behind the towels; you even checked that room filled with all the other safes. May we recommend slipping on a pair of X-ray Goggles? Sure, you'll see skeletons instead of your colleagues. Get over it, my friend! They're just bones. We've all got them. And anyway, how else are you going to discover that the secret safe is actually hidden in that upper-right kitchen cabinet behind the super-size jug of off-brand ketchup?

Pro: Find hidden things quickly.

Con: OMG, we can see your skeleton and it's freaking us out!

Wristwatch

This crazy device is beyond your wildest imagination. You know how cell phones always show the correct time of day? You just click one of those buttons on the phone, and the time pops up in easy-to-read digital numerals. Well, prepare to have your mind blown. We want you to picture a device that can tell you the time without being in your pocket—strapped instead around your very own wrist. So instead of digging out your phone, all you have to do is rotate your wrist and—*BAM!*—you can see the time. Crazy, right?

Now picture this: Instead of telling you the time in numbers—which any nearby super villain would be able to see and understand all too easily—this "watch" utilizes a complex circular code. You picturing this? Because that is exactly what we've got here. One through twelve are labeled around the edges. Through twelve! How sneaky is that? And three tiny sticks rotate obscurely, and only the people who are able to read these sticks can know the time by looking at this gadget.

And to top it all off, the whole thing is powered by gears. Gears! The world may never be the same.

Of course, we here at the Anti-Villain League were not merely content with this groundbreaking piece of wizardry. We have added several modifications to this device, even though we didn't need to because it is already so cool. Turn the page for a short list.

Pro: No one else knows what time it is.

Con: Strap may chafe or pull your arm hair.

Watch Modifications

1. Shoots foam at an adversary (say, an attack chicken, for instance). This foam then instantly hardens into a ball around the torso of said attack chicken, totally immobilizing it. This also turns it into a reasonable facsimile of a bowling ball, if you happen to be in need of one.

2. Shoots moose tranquilizers. These powerful tranquilizers can easily save your partner from a humiliating date without anyone knowing what happened. What? You've never seen someone take a nap on their plate of spaghetti and meatballs before?

3. Eavesdropping device. Hear what someone is saying across a crowded room. Maybe they are talking about you!

We would like to engineer more modifications to this cutting-edge device. (Did we mention the gears?) Please use the space below to brainstorm a few new functions and super gadget upgrades we can offer.*

_____

_____

_____

_____

_____

_____

*Not that we need to because it's really cool already without any modifications at all.

Microscopic Transmitter

You know how transmitters used to be so big and everything? Well, those days are over. This transmitter is so small, it's invisible to the human eye. You can't even be sure you are holding one in your hand! We're talking an infinitesimal device. Pick it up carefully—try pinching it between your thumb and index finger. Are you holding it? Who knows? You probably are. Now carefully place it in your ear, but be sure not to lose it inside there. Those things are expensive.

Pro: Virtually undetectable.

Con: We keep losing them down agents' ear canals.

Purse Glider

Have you ever carried a purse? Have you ever wished you had a hang glider? Well, finally, you can have it all. This fashionable, sturdy, useful bag looks great, has tons of interior space for carrying everything you need, and easily transforms into a huge hang glider by pulling a hidden cord. There is even a little zippy pocket inside the bag for your phone and a couple of pens or something. Maybe even a pack of gum. And this way, next time you pop the door on a high-flying jet and leap into the rushing air at a dizzying height, you will be so prepared.

Pro: Cute AND useful.

Con: Haven't figured out where your stuff should go once the purse converts to the hang glider.

Nanobot Universal Key

This handy-dandy gadget is quite possibly the most intricate invention we have ever inventified over at the Anti-Villain League. Microscopic particles on the key automatically rearrange themselves to open any lock known to man, woman, child, or beast.

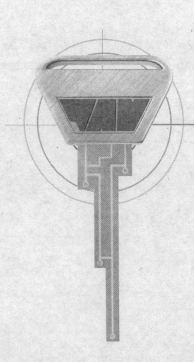

Speaking of rearranging particles, perhaps we could engage your assistance here in rearranging some letters, particularly the letters in the words "Nanobot Universal Key." As part of your screening process, we would like to see how many new words you can make with these letters. More than thirty may just get our attention, possible Agent What's-Your-Name.

NANOBOT UNIVERSAL KEY

_____   _____
_____   _____
_____   _____
_____   _____
_____   _____
_____   _____
_____   _____
_____   _____
_____   _____
_____   _____
_____   _____

Debriefing

Thank you for your interest in the Anti-Villain League! Since we have already scanned your entire chemical profile into our database, there's no possible place you can ever hide from us now. If we want to find you, we'll find you all right. And if we want to talk to you, we'll do our best to remember to choose Invitation Option 2 (but we're not promising anything!).

Farewell until then. And remember: Always check for laser-beam alarm triggers. And hidden wires attached to bells on doors. And attack chickens.

MEE MO MEEE MO

Uh-oh—our serum sensors seem to have picked up a new trail. No time left to waste on an AVL tutorial for a civilian like you. We hope you've learned enough to get you started on your new non–super villain career.

See you if we want to. Toodle, pip, and cheerio!

Pages 28-29: Semaphorically Speaking puzzle

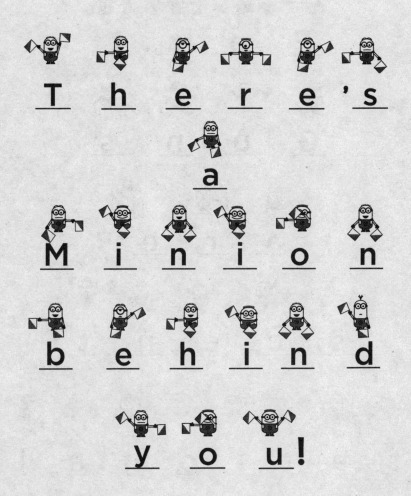

T h e r e ' s

a

M i n i o n

b e h i n d

y o u !

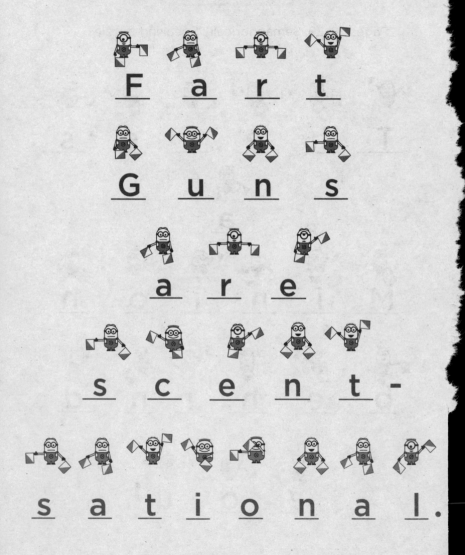

F a r t

G u n s

a r e

s c e n t -

s a t i o n a l .